MATCHBOX
HERO·CITY

Off-Road
RESCUE

By Annie Auerbach
Illustrated by Artful Doodlers Ltd.

LITTLE SIMON
New York   London   Toronto   Sydney

LITTLE SIMON

An imprint of Simon & Schuster Children's Publishing Division

1230 Avenue of the Americas

New York, New York 10020

Copyright © 2004 Mattel, Inc. MATCHBOX and all associated logos are trademarks

owned by and used under license from Mattel, Inc. All rights reserved.

LITTLE SIMON and colophon are registered trademarks of Simon & Schuster.

All rights reserved, including the right of reproduction in whole or in part in any form.

Manufactured in the United States of America

First Edition

2   4   6   8   10   9   7   5   3   1

ISBN 0-689-86727-1

"Woo-hoo!" Kevin yelled as he whipped around a corner.

Kevin revved the engine of his four-wheel all-terrain vehicle.
Gripping the handlebars, he started to go over some rough terrain.

Suddenly the ATV spun out. Kevin tried to regain control. But the
terrain won.

"Oh, man!" Kevin said, realizing the ATV was stuck. He got off the vehicle and *squish*! He had stepped in mud up to his knees.

Kevin had only recently discovered how amazing off-roading on the hidden trails in the mountains was. Now he got paid to be out here because he was a member of the mountain search-and-rescue squad. Even on his day off, you could find him out here . . . usually covered in mud!

Kevin pulled out a jack and was able to lift the ATV up. Then he stuffed some rocks and shrubbery under the wheels and soon got the vehicle out of the mud. His shift started in a few hours, so he'd just head to work to get changed.

At the ranger station Kevin was greeted by his teammates.

"Is that you under there?" joked Brett, the team leader.

"Kevin, what's that smell?" teased Erin. "*Eau de mud* perfume?"

"Ha, ha. Very funny," said Kevin, rolling his eyes. "Have you considered a career in comedy?"

The others went back to work, trying not to laugh, and Kevin went to shower and change his clothes.

Soon a call came through dispatch. A woman had phoned to report her husband missing. He went out for a bike ride early that morning, but should have been back already.

"He went up toward Moose Creek," Brett reported to the others. "A helicopter crew already went up, but they couldn't spot anything. Erin and Kevin, take the SUV with the ATVs up and see what you can find."

The rescue squad used special vehicles to get into areas where other vehicles could not go. With mostly narrow dirt roads and trails in the mountains, there were few roads up there.

"I'll drive," said Erin. "Let's go!"

The SUV sped off up the one paved road toward Moose Creek.

"I don't see anyone," said Kevin, looking around. "Maybe the rider got to Moose Creek and tried to take the shortcut back."

"You mean the shortcut that isn't really a shortcut?" asked Erin.

"Yup," replied Kevin. "Let's pull over and check it out."

As Erin radioed dispatch what their status was, Kevin unloaded the ATVs from the trailer. Then they both hopped on the four-wheelers and took off down the steep ravine.

The big, wide tires on the ATVs gripped the terrain as they sped down the rocky path. There was no time to lose!

In the distance something yellow caught Erin's eye. "I see something," she yelled. As she got closer she realized the yellow coloring was a sweatshirt.

They had found the cyclist, but he was lying on the ground! Leaping off her ATV, Erin checked to see if the man was okay. She was a trained emergency technician and was invaluable in rescue situations.

"Oh! Thank heavens!" said the cyclist, as Erin helped him to his feet. "I'm not sure what happened. The bike must have hit a loose rock, and I landed flat on my back!"

"Dispatch," Kevin said into his radio, "we've found the cyclist."

The cyclist seemed to be fine, just shaken up a bit. Together Kevin and Erin took him and his bike out of the ravine and back to the SUV.

During that fall season the squad performed many rescues. Before long, fall turned to winter and brought with it the first snowfall of the season.

"It's so beautiful," Erin said. "I love it when it snows."

"Yes," said Brett. "But just remember what else comes with the snow— overexcited skiers! I predict we're going to have a busy rescue season."

Erin knew Brett was right. Snow definitely made their job more challenging.

Within hours the first rescue call came in: some injured skiers on the side of Mount Pepe, one of the highest and most difficult ski runs. It's an area only the most experienced skiers should ski. But amateurs liked to try it despite the danger.

This was a job for the whole team. They drove up to Mount Pepe, hauling behind them the only vehicles that would get the job done—the snowmobiles.

When they got to their destination, they unloaded the snowmobiles and rescue sleds and quickly set up a base area. The Mountain Medic Team met them there and the two teams worked together.

Brett was the team leader and gave the orders. "Kevin and Erin, you take the switchback trail. The guys from the Medic Team will follow you with the rescue sleds. Let's find those skiers—and fast!"

Kevin and Erin took the lead. Speed was important but so was safety.
Each person knew how to use a snowmobile to its full capacity. They made
up a swift unit, navigating through the heavily forested area.

Kevin and Erin drove their snowmobiles down the narrow paths, cutting through the snow. They steered using the handlebars, which controlled ski-like devices on the front of the vehicle. They also made sure to lean into each turn for maximum speed.

"Help! Help! We're over here!" came a voice up ahead. It was one of the skiers! Kevin eased up on the throttle and motioned for Erin and the others to slow down and then stop.

Quickly the team worked to check the status of the skiers.

"Two out of the three seem to be injured," Erin said after she and the Medic Team took a quick look. "Good thing we've got the rescue sleds."

Kevin radioed to Brett back at the base area. "We've got 'em. We're going to transport them out of this area. They need medical attention."

"Good work," Brett replied. "I'll radio dispatch for a helicopter to transfer them from the base area to the hospital."

Before long the injured skiers were strapped into the rescue sleds. The third skier sat behind Kevin on his snowmobile. By the time the rescue teams completed their journey back to the base station, the helicopter had arrived. Soon the snowmobiles were loaded back onto the trailers and it was time to head back to the station.

"Thanks for your assistance," Brett told the medics.

"It's our job," one of the medics replied. "I'm sure we'll see you soon."

Brett sighed. "You can count on it—as long as there's snow on these mountains!"

Erin, Brett, and Kevin pulled back into the ranger station. A light snow began to fall as they got out of the SUV.

Erin and Brett were tired, but saving people always energized Kevin. "Anyone up for some off-roading after our shift?"

Erin and Brett looked at each other and winked. Then they pelted Kevin with snowballs!

"What did I say?" he said with a laugh as he ran for cover.